First Edition, April 2018
10 9 8 7 6 5 4 3 2 1
FAC-029191-18047
Printed in Malaysia
The lettering for this book was created by the author, based on
Century Schoolbook Pro/Monotype.
Designed by Joann Hill and Greg Pizzoli. Printed in five spot colors.
Illustrations created with pencil and Photoshop.

Library of Congress Cataloging-in-Publication Data

Names: Pizzoli, Greg, author, illustrator.
Title: This story is for you / Greg Pizzoli.
Description: First edition. • Los Angeles ; New York : Disney-Hyperion, 2018.
Summary: Illustrations and easy-to-read text celebrate a friendship
that recognizes what makes one person special and guarantees a closeness
that will last through time and across distance.
Identifiers: LCCN 2017036129 • ISBN 9781484750308 (hardcover) •
ISBN 1484750306 (hardcover)
Subjects: CYAC: Individuality—Fiction. • Friendship—Fiction. •
Imagination—Fiction. • BISAC: JUVENILE FICTION / Social Issues /
Friendship. • JUVENILE FICTION / Imagination & Play.
Classification: LCC PZ7.P6898 Thi 2018 • DDC [E]—dc23
LC record available at https://lccn.loc.gov/2017036129

Reinforced binding
Visit www.DisneyBooks.com

This Story
Is For You

Greg Pizzoli

Disney • HYPERION ✳ Los Angeles • New York

This story is for you.
You and only you.

You're the only one
in the world with
your eyes . . .

your nose,

your fingers,

and
your
smile.

And if we meet one day,
I'll see you and say . . .

"It's nice to know you."

We can play games,
and make shadows on the wall,
and sing songs we make up
on the spot.

I'M A
BUMBLEBEE
FEE LA LA...

I'M A
WATERFALL
LA LA FEE...

We'll write letters to the moon,
and stay up as late as we can,
and I'll save you the last candy
that you really like.

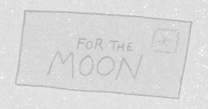

Maybe one day,
a long, long time from now,
you will leave
and go someplace new.

And you will take a trip,
and go a long, long way,

and come to a place where
you've never been.

You will meet some people
and animals, too—

But you'll be
the only one
just like you.

The only one
with your ears,

your toes,

your laugh,

and
your
smile.

And if I found a map,
and a ship to sail to you,
I would sail a long, long way
just looking for you.

And when I'm alone
with the stars
and the moonlight,
the same moonlight
we've always known,
I won't feel alone;
I'll be with you.

And if I pass a ship,
I'll turn toward the light,
and wave in the darkness
to say that I know you.

And if I found you,
after such a long, long time,
I would give you a big, long hug,
and hold you, and smell you,
and say . . .

I've traveled far
and waited long
and met many people, too,
but in all the world,
you're the only one
just like you.

You're the only one with

your eyes,

your nose,

your fingers,

and
your
smile.

You are my friend,
and it's nice to know you.